Wheedle
on the Needle

Written by **Stephen Cosgrove**
Illustrated by **Robin James**

First Sasquatch Books edition
Originally published by Serendipity Press, 1974
Revised edition published by Price Stern Sloan, a division of Penguin Putnam Inc., 2002

Manufactured in China in January 2012 by C&C Offset Printing Co. Ltd. Shenzhen, Guangdong Province
Published by Sasquatch Books

15 14 13 12   10 9 8 7 6 5

Cover design: Rosebud Eustace
Cover and interior illustrations: Robin James
Interior design and composition: Rosebud Eustace

Library of Congress Cataloging-in-Publication Data

Cosgrove, Stephen.
  Wheedle on the Needle / written by Stephen Cosgrove ; illustrated by Robin James. -- 1st Sasquatch Books ed.
      p. cm.
  Summary: A Wheedle goes to great lengths to prevent the people of Seattle from disturbing his sleep.
  ISBN-13: 978-1-57061-628-0
  ISBN-10: 1-57061-628-0
  [1. Sleep--Fiction. 2. Seattle (Wash.)--Fiction.] I. James, Robin, 1953- ill. II. Title.
  PZ7.C8187Wh 2009
  [E]--dc22

                              2009025269

Sasquatch Books
1904 Third Avenue, Suite 710
Seattle, WA 98101
(206) 467-4300
www.sasquatchbooks.com
custserv@sasquatchbooks.com

One day in 1974 I set my mind to creating a story about and for Seattle. Using the Space Needle as a background, I began the creative process. Fortunately and unfortunately, the only word I could think of that rhymed with Needle was Wheedle. Later that day as I walked in a quiet rain, the peace and tranquility of the moment was shattered by a loud whistle from a ferry on the Sound. Of these tiny seeds the story was sown.

The book was dedicated then and is rededicated now to Seattle.

—Stephen Cosgrove

Many, many years ago, before explorers sailed to the Northwest, there lived a large, happy creature called the Wheedle.

He was pleasingly plump, covered in orange fluffy fur, and had a big round, red nose.

He spent his days sniffing flowers and enjoying the peace and quiet that nature offered.

Forever and a day everything was peaceful, until one afternoon the Wheedle watched curiously as a large ship sailed into the bay.

Laughing loudly, workers jumped from the ship and set about clearing the land and building this, that, and other things. As they worked they whistled, and the more they worked, the more they whistled.

All that whistling hurt the poor Wheedle's ears.

The whistling continued night and day, and the Wheedle could get absolutely no sleep at all.

With no sleep he became grouchier and grouchier.

If he was ever to get some sleep, the Wheedle knew he must put a stop to all this whistling.

"Hmm," he thought, "if the workers don't have their tools, they won't be able to work and if they can't work, they won't whistle!"

So later that night he sneaked into the workers' camp and took all of their tools.

Sadly for the Wheedle, the next morning the men quickly got new tools from the ship and went back to work, whistling even louder than before.

If anything, the Wheedle was resourceful. He decided that the next best thing to do was to scare the workers. For when workers are scared they can't pucker, and when they can't pucker, they can't whistle. As we all know, a puckerless whistle is no whistle at all.

One by one he began creeping up behind them and growling at the top of his voice. Sure enough, the workers were so scared that they couldn't whistle a whit.

All would have been the Wheedle's salvation, save for one brave lumberjack, who, to prove he wasn't scared, simply whistled.

The Wheedle put his hands over his ears and ran into the forest.

Well, let me tell you, that did it! The Wheedle knew he could no longer live near the bay. So he packed his belongings and left.

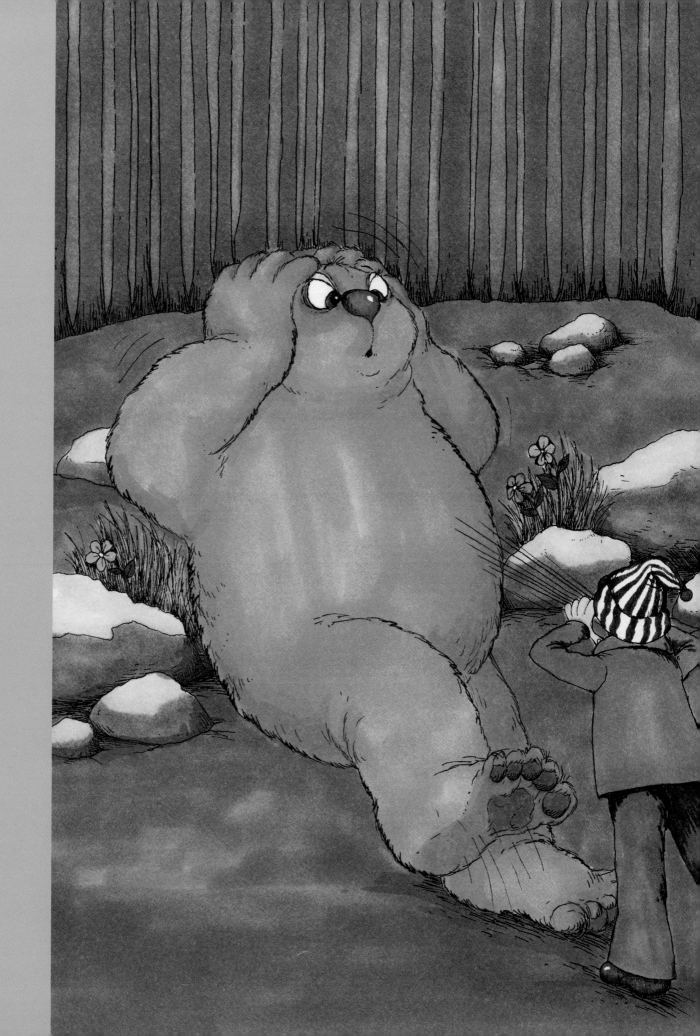

He wandered high into the mountains searching for a place far enough away from the workers that he wouldn't hear the whistling. He wandered and wandered until he came to the very top of Mount Rainier.

He listened very carefully. What delight! He couldn't hear even a whisper of a whistle on the wind.

He quickly unpacked his sleeping sack, his toothbrush with the squiggly on the end, and his white, woolly pajamas.

This was the quiet place he had hoped for. This was a place where he could sleep for a long, long time.

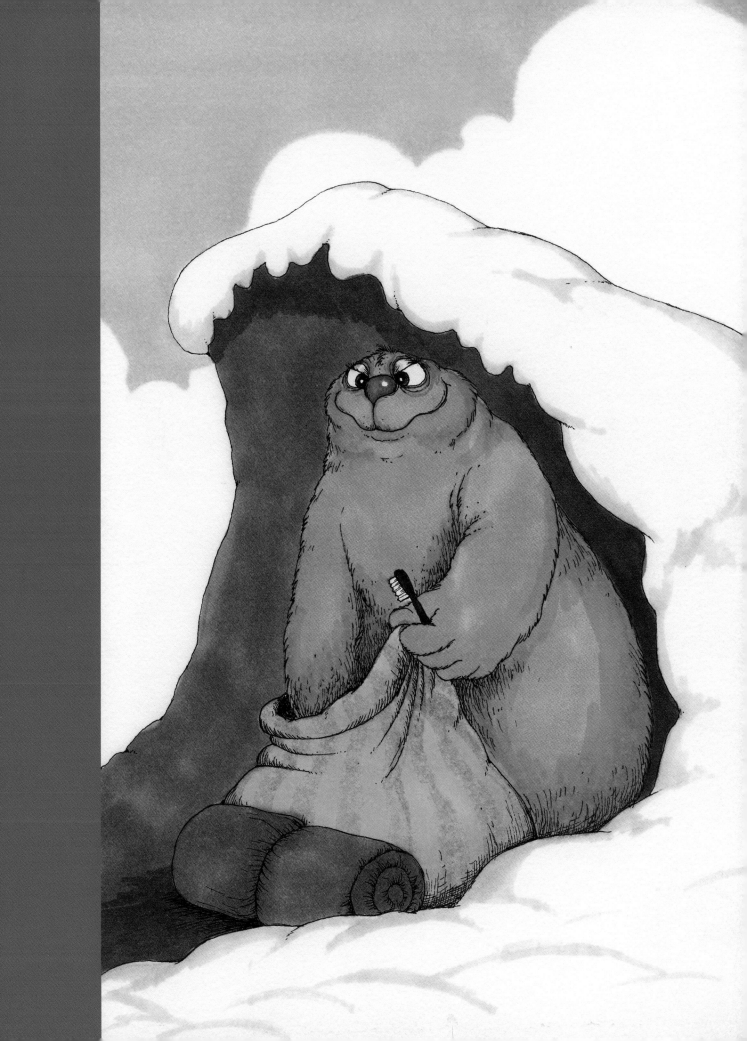

He quickly brushed his teeth, washed his furry hands, and slipped into his woolly pajamas. Then, he slid his big body into the sleeping sack, flopped his head on his pillow, and fell fast asleep.

He was so happy in his deep sleep that his big red nose blinked on and off like a flashing beacon on a tall pole.

He slept through the night, through the day, through weeks and months, and on through several years.

Oh, such sweet, sweet dreams.

But, after a long while something woke the Wheedle from his deep sleep.

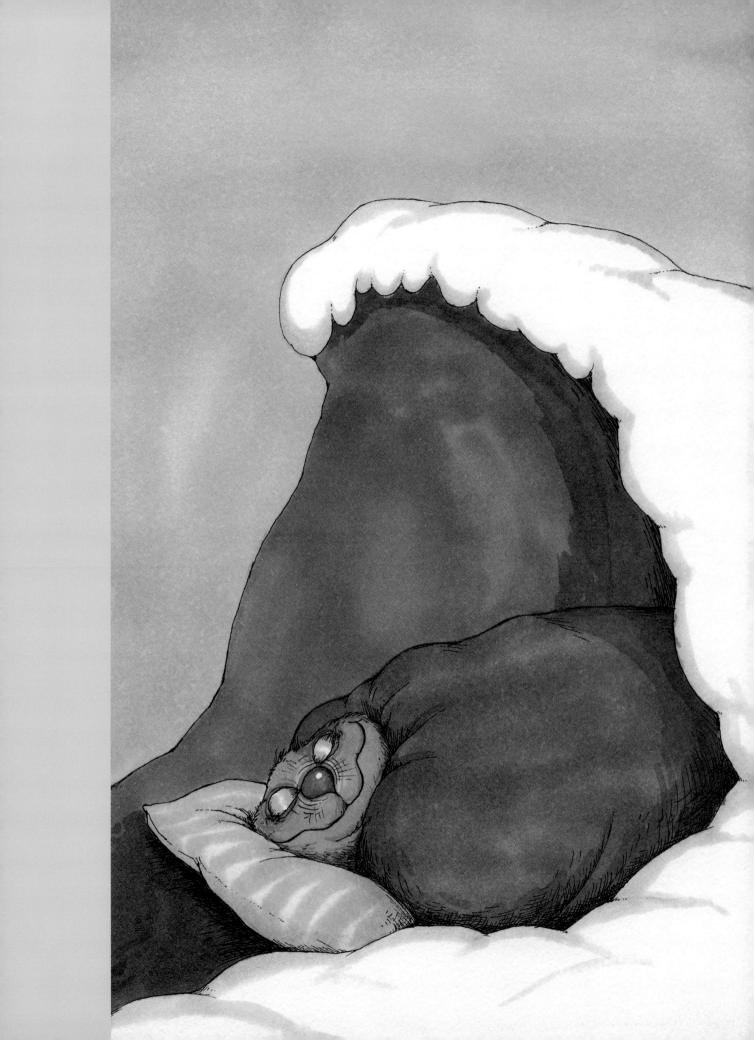

Whistling!
Loud whistling!
Happy whistling!

He looked about and much to his surprise, he saw that the workers had continued to build over the years and now had built almost to the edge of his mountain. But what was more alarming was that now everybody was whistling, children and workers alike.

"Oh, no!" cried the Wheedle. "What am I ever to do? With all this whistling I'll never get back to sleep!"

He began pacing up and down the mountain, mumbling and grumbling all the while.

Then his nose lit up and a smile crossed his lips.

"I've got it!" he chuckled. And with that he removed everything from his large striped bag and with it dragging behind, he climbed to the very top of Mount Rainier. He stood on his fuzzy tiptoes, reached up into the sky, and grabbed a cloud. Then he grabbed another and another.

One by one he stuffed the clouds into the bag until he had it full to overflowing.

With the bag thrown over his shoulder he set out for the source of his noisy-whistling problem, the growing city of Seattle.

The skyline of the city was filled with tall buildings, but the Wheedle only needed one to complete his plan.

And the one he chose was the Space Needle.

Giddy to put his plan in action, he hurried to the base of the Space Needle, jumped into the elevator, and zipped to the very top. There he stood and looked about. All around were happy children and workers all whistling and laughing, having a great time.

The Wheedle chuckled as he reached deep into the soggy bag. He grabbed a fluffy cloud by the tail and then slung it around and around and flipped it into the air. The cloud lifted high into the sky and then hung there like a glop of whipped cream on a blue kitchen ceiling. The cloud gurgled and sloshed, and then one drop of rain fell and then another and another. Soon it was pouring.

Now, the kindly folks in Seattle like the rain, but it is nearly impossible and highly improbable that one can whistle with any intensity in a rainstorm. With the rain falling all around, everyone ran inside and soon it became very still, very quiet, indeed.

The Wheedle stretched out on the top of the Space Needle and, using the bag of clouds as a pillow, fell fast asleep.

With each snarkled snore his big red nose slowly blinked on and off.

And as he slept it rained and it rained . . .

. . . and it rained. The people of Seattle had to stay inside and they became very sad.

It didn't take much to figure out that someone was throwing clouds into the sky from the top of the Space Needle.

Finally, the mayor himself went to the Wheedle on the Needle to plead with him to stop throwing rain clouds into the sky.

"Please," said the mayor, "would you stop throwing clouds into the sky? The kindly folk of Seattle love to whistle while they work, but with all the rain, there is little to whistle about, and without whistling there is little work being done."

The Wheedle said he was sorry, but still and all he couldn't sleep when he heard whistling. There was nothing he could do.

Now the mayor thought and thought and quickly devised a plan, a wonderful plan indeed.

The mayor's plan was a simple plan, and sometimes simplicity is best.

All through the night and into the next morning, sail makers stitched and sewed cotton, flannel, and wool. Miles of thread were laced through the eyes of needles as the weathered hands of the sail makers sewed. They sewed pink flannel onto yellow wool, and blue cotton onto red flannel, and by early morning they had finished their task.

Who ever said that mayors never think a thoughtful thought?

This was a good plan. This plan was great.

At precisely noon, not a minute before and not a minute after, the mayor again met with the Wheedle on the Needle. In his hands he held the largest pair of earmuffs you have ever seen.

"These earmuffs are for you," said the mayor in his most political of voices. "With these on your ears you won't hear a thing. You won't hear us whistle. You won't even hear the big whistles from the ships in the harbor or the trains going by."

The Wheedle pulled the earmuffs over his ears and was surrounded in the delight of silence. He didn't hear the kindly folk of Seattle cheering. He didn't hear the end of the mayor's speech. With the earmuffs in place, he simply rolled over and fell fast asleep.

So content was he that his big red nose again began to blink.

There's a Wheedle on the Needle
I know just what you're thinking,
But if you look up late at night
You'll see his red nose blinking.

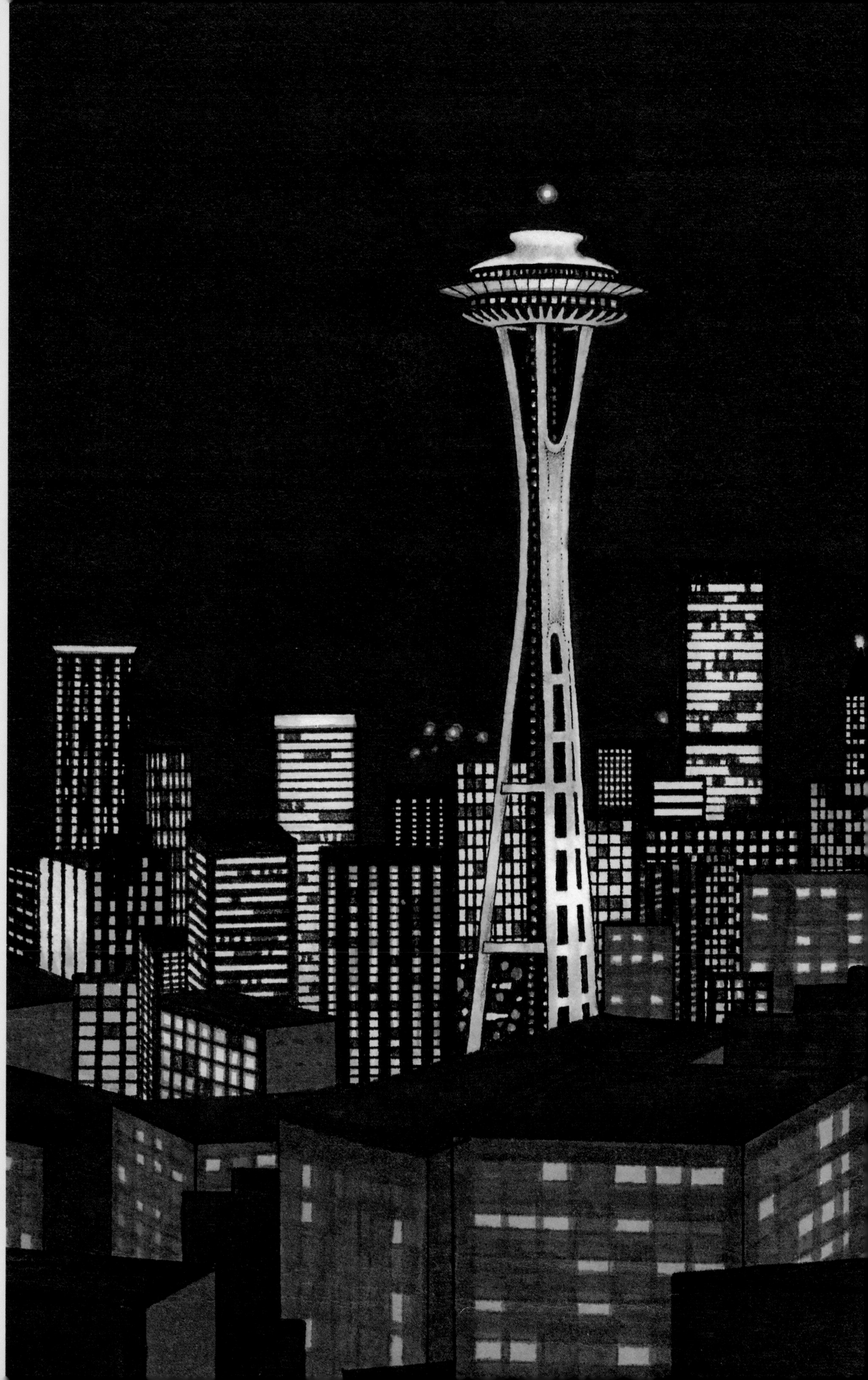

About the Author

I have spent my life as a dream-maker. To be able to crawl inside a story as it is being created is an unbelievable and delightful experience. By reading this book and others that I have written, you are able to share my experiences. I have written and published 320 books or so, and it is only by the grace of God that I continue this amazing adventure.

—Stephen Cosgrove

About the Illustrator

I have been drawing since I could hold a pencil.

After illustrating 82 books over the past 35 years, I realize there is no greater joy than doing what I love and knowing it may bring a smile to someone's face. It's the icing on the cake of life.

—Robin James